THE STARS AND STRIPES

Stars and stripes first appeared on American flags in 1775. Not until June 14, 1777, however, did the Continental Congress, the American government at that time, decide what the flag should look like. The Congress decided "the flag of the 13 United States be 13 stripes, alternate red and white; the union be thirteen stars, white in a blue field, representing a new constellation."

On May 1, 1795, Congress passed a new act giving the flag fifteen stripes and fifteen stars. Congress passed a third act on April 4, 1818, stating that "the flag of the United States be thirteen horizontal stripes, alternate red and white . . . that on the admission of every new State into the Union, one star be added to the union of the flag." This law remains in effect today.

The flag was nicknamed "Old Glory" in 1831 by William Driver, captain of an American ship, *Charles Daggett*. On May 30, 1916, President Woodrow Wilson established June 14 as Flag Day, a national holiday.

This book contains fifteen American flags, including our current "Old Glory."

STARS & STRIPES

OUR NATIONAL FLAG

written and illustrated by

LEONARD EVERETT FISHER

Holiday House / New York

To Margery and that wonderful, lovable gang of ours,
Julie and Robert; Susan, Judah, and Sam; Pamela and James;
and the rest of us yet unborn.

frontispiece:

Great Star, 1818   Following the passage of the Flag Act of April 4, 1818, this banner with twenty stars was hoisted over the capitol dome on April 13, 1818. The design was changed later that year to five horizontal and four vertical rows of stars.

opposite:

South Carolina Navy, 1775–1781   The naval forces of South Carolina used this flag during the Revolutionary War.

Copyright © 1993 by Leonard Everett Fisher
Printed in the United States of America
All rights reserved
FIRST EDITION
Library of Congress Cataloging-in-Publication Data
Fisher, Leonard Everett.
Stars and stripes: our national flag / Leonard Everett Fisher. — 1st ed.
p.   cm.
Summary: With the Pledge of Allegiance as accompanying text,
presents various American flags and gives brief historical information about each.
ISBN 0-8234-1053-6
1. United States—History—Revolution. 1775–1783—Flags—Juvenile literature. 2. Flags—United States—
History—Juvenile literature. 3. Bellamy, Francis. Pledge of allegiance to the flag—Juvenile literature. [1. Flags—United
States—History. 2. Pledge of Allegiance. 3. United States—History—Revolution, 1775–1783— Flags.] I. Title.
E289.F57   1993   93-20176   CIP   AC
973.7—dc20

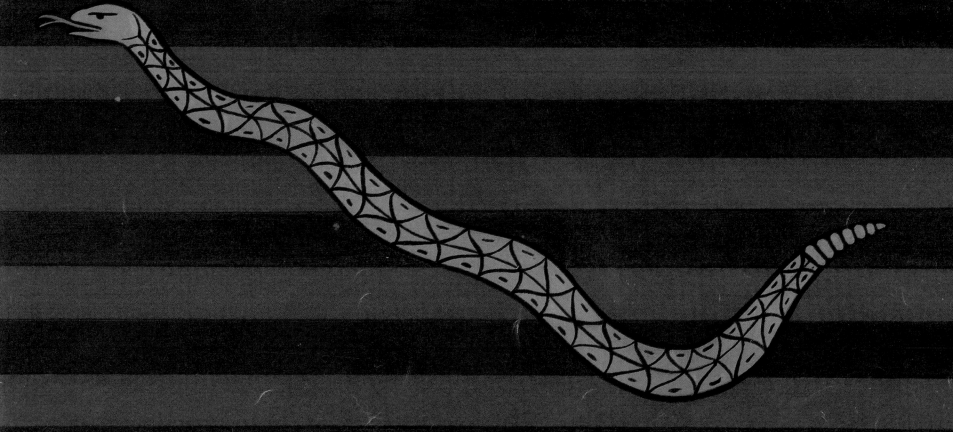

I

Green Mountain Boys, 1775 Vermont's fighting men carried this banner at Cambridge, Massachusetts, July 3, 1775, when George Washington took command of America's unorganized forces.

pledge

Grand Union, 1776–1777 General George Washington had this flag raised at Somerville, Massachusetts, January 1, 1776, on the day America's Continental Army was formed. The colonists placed six white stripes on the solid red field of the British naval flag. The thirteen red and white stripes stood for the thirteen colonies.

allegiance

Hopkinson Design, 1777–1780 Francis Hopkinson, a signer of the Declaration of Independence, asked the Continental Congress to consider this design after it called for a national flag.

to the Flag

Vermont Militia, 1777 Known as the "Bennington Flag," this banner was seen during the Battle of Bennington, Vermont, on August 16, 1777. It is thought to be the first "Stars and Stripes" to be flown during a land battle.

of the United States of America,

Betsy Ross, 1777–1795 Legend has it that Betsy Ross, a Philadelphia seamstress, sewed this flag after George Washington presented her with a design.

and to the Republic

Serapis, 1779   American Captain John Paul Jones hoisted this flag over the British warship, HMS *Serapis,* after capturing it during the Revolutionary War, September 23, 1779.

for which it stands,

Alliance, 1779   The flag of the USS *Alliance,* one of the ships in Captain John Paul Jones's fleet.

one Nation

Third Maryland Regiment, 1781–1846   This flag was carried by Maryland troops in the Battle of Cowpens, South Carolina, January 17, 1781.

under God,

North Carolina Militia, 1781   Soldiers from North Carolina carried this flag in the Battle of Guilford Courthouse, North Carolina, March 15, 1781.

indivisible,

Star-Spangled Banner, 1812–1814   In 1812, America entered into another war against the English. This fifteen-star, fifteen-stripe flag was flown as the British bombarded Fort McHenry, Baltimore, Maryland, September 13–14, 1814. It inspired Francis Scott Key to write America's national anthem, "The Star-Spangled Banner."

with liberty

Pathfinder, 1842–1848 Captain John C. Frémont carried this flag when he explored territory west of the Rocky Mountains.

and justice

Fort Sumter, 1861 At the outbreak of the Civil War, April 12, 1861, this flag flew over Fort Sumter, in the harbor of Charleston, South Carolina.

for all.

Old Glory, 1960–present The fifty-star flag of the United States of America has existed since July 4, 1960, after Alaska and Hawaii became states in 1959.

The Pledge of Allegiance

The Pledge of Allegiance was first recited in the fall of 1892. President Benjamin Harrison had proclaimed a National School Celebration to mark the four hundreth anniversary of the voyage of Christopher Columbus to the Western Hemisphere. Francis Bellamy, an editor of *The Youth's Companion,* in Boston, Massachusetts, thought every American schoolchild should make a solemn promise of loyalty to the United States to mark the occasion. With that in mind he wrote a "Pledge of Allegiance."

In 1923, and again in 1924, the American Legion slightly lengthened the original version. In 1942, after the United States entered the Second World War, Congress passed a law stating rules for the use of the flag. These included the now familiar Pledge of Allegiance. Twelve years later, in 1954, Congress added two words to The Pledge of Allegiance that had not been there before—"under God."